ONE HUNDRED BONES!

To little Noya, welcome to the world,
with all my love - Y.Z.

A TEMPLAR BOOK

First published in the UK in 2015 by Templar Publishing,
an imprint of the Bonnier Company Limited,
Deepdene Lodge, Deepdene Avenue, Dorking, Surrey, RH5 4AT, UK
www.templarco.co.uk

Copyright © 2015 by Yuval Zommer

10 9 8 7 6 5 4 3 2 1

ISBN 978-1-78370-279-4 (hardback)
ISBN 978-1-78370-351-7 (paperback)

Designed by Genevieve Webster
Edited by Zanna Davidson

Printed in China

One Hundred Bones!

Yuval Zommer

templar publishing

Scruff was not like other dogs.

He didn't wear a collar.
His fur was never brushed.
He didn't even have a human friend
saying things like, "Stay!" or "Sit!"
or "Good Boy!"

KEEP OFF THE GRASS!

NO DOGS ALLOWED

When Percy the pug, Pixie the poodle, Sidney the sausage dog and Ada the Afghan were all out on their walkies, Scruff got on with doing what he did best – digging

and digging

and digging . . .

The other dogs were NOT impressed. Nor were their human friends.

"Stop digging up my flowerbeds!" Mrs Fancypants cried.

"Get off my lawn!" Mr Fusspot warned.

"Not you again!" Mr Greenfingers called.

"Shoo! Shoo! Go away!" huffed Mrs Hoity-Toity.

So Scruff set off in search of a friendlier place.

He went further than he'd ever been before, way beyond the fields,

through the woods,

and over the distant hills,

as he followed the most awesome smell.

And when he found it, he began to dig.

Deep, deep down into the ground,

tunnelling and burrowing until he reached . . .

the biggest pile of bones he had ever seen.

There were tiny bones,
mighty bones,

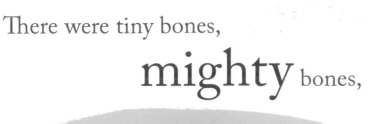

thin little twig bones,

strange-shaped funny bones,

and bones the size of **trees!**

"Ten bones, twenty bones,
thirty bones . . . Cor!
Forty bones, fifty bones,
sixty bones and more!"

And away Scruff ran
back over the hills,
through the woods,
across the fields,
and into town.

"Please come and **help** me dig!"
he begged.

"But my nose would get dirty!" said Pixie.

"What about my hair?" sniffed Ada.

"My paws would get muddy!" protested Percy.

"This could get me into serious trouble . . ." said Sidney.

"Fine!" said Scruff. "I'll keep the bones to myself then!"

"Did you say bones?"
barked the other dogs. "Where?"

"Follow me!" cried Scruff.

One hundred bones later, they still weren't sure exactly what it was they'd uncovered.

"You don't see bones like these in the butchers," said Scruff.

"Or in the supermarket," added Ada.

"They're not like the ones I get from the restaurant," said Pixie.
"And they're even bigger than the bones I get
for Christmas!" cried Sidney.
"Hmm," said Percy. "I think I know
where I've seen bones
like these before!"

So they went underground,

overground, and all the way
across town to . . .

BUS STOP
28

28 SOUTH KENSINGTON

. . . the Natural History Museum!

"Well, well, well," said Professor Dinovsky.

"What have we got here?"

"Extraordinary! Magnificent! Amazing!
This could be the most exciting discovery of our time!"

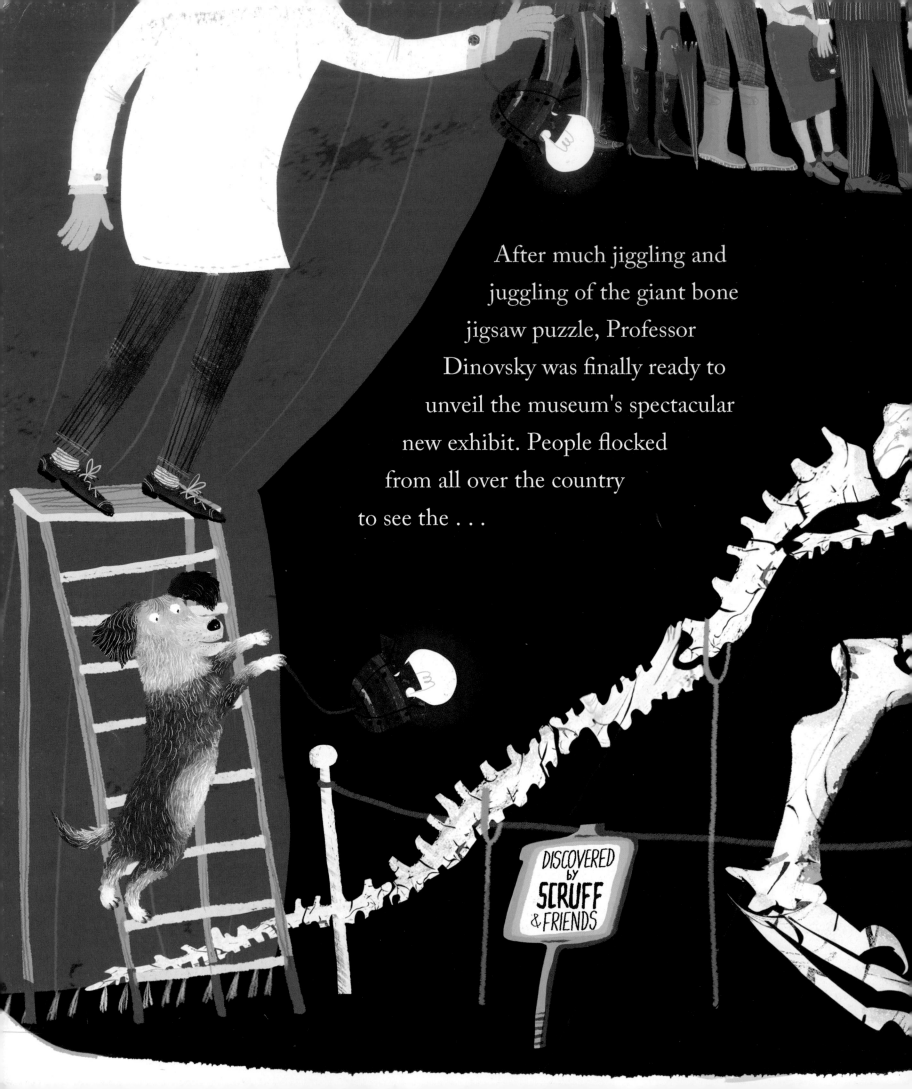

After much jiggling and juggling of the giant bone jigsaw puzzle, Professor Dinovsky was finally ready to unveil the museum's spectacular new exhibit. People flocked from all over the country to see the . . .

DISCOVERED by SCRUFF & FRIENDS

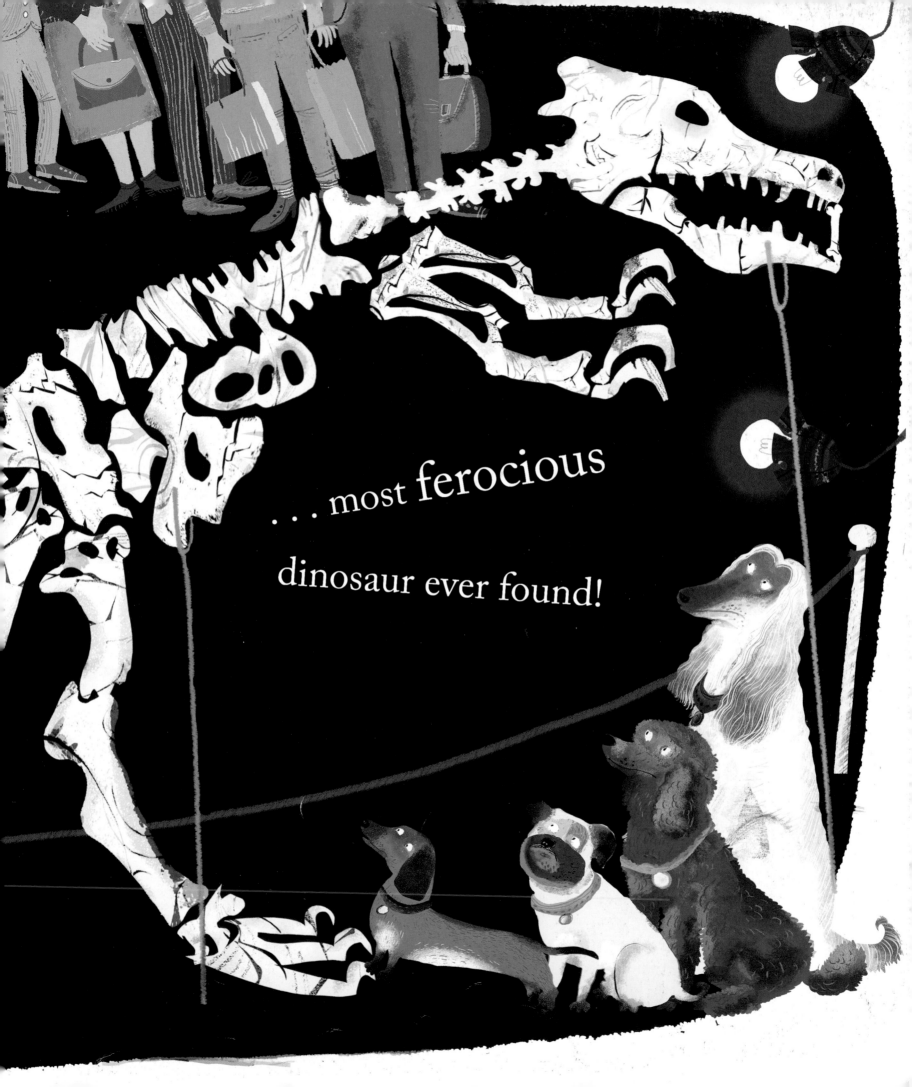

. . . most ferocious

dinosaur ever found!

There was a special ceremony and Scruff was given a shiny gold medal. He even got his picture on the front page of the paper.

THE DAILY BARK

DOG HAS HIS DAY!

TOP DIGGER

But best of all, Scruff finally found a home . . .

. . . and a human friend all of his own.

And he still got
to **dig!**

THE
END

Scruff the dog just loves to dig.

He's also raggedy and homeless and a little bit lonely.
Until the day he finds not ten . . . not twenty . . . but ONE HUNDRED BONES!
What could they be?

An exciting and heart-warming tale of discovery and friendship for dog
and dinosaur-lovers everywhere.

Also by Yuval Zommer:

£6.99

ISBN 978-1-78370-351-7

9 781783 703517

Printed in China

templar publishing
www.templarco.co.uk

ISBN: Hardback 978-1-84877-772-9 Softback 978-1-84877-760-6